MIDSUMMER MURDER
MOTHER EARTHS KITCHEN
COZY MYSTERY SERIES
BOOK 7

PBODI

99 Cent Press

All trademarks and brands referred to in this book are for illustrative purposes only, are the property of their respective owners and not affiliated with this publication in any way. Any trademarks are being used without permission, and the publication of the trademark is not authorized by, associated with or sponsored by the trademark owner.

MIDSUMMER MURDER
First Printing November 2016
Published by:
99 Cent Press
http://www.99CentPress.com
Printed in the United States of America

New Year's Resolution

The Heart Of The Murder

The Luck Of The Irish

A Corpse In The Kitchen

Midsummer Murder

Mother Earth's Kitchen Box Set Books 1-4

Mother Earth's Kitchen Box Set Books 5-7

Mother Earth's Kitchen Box Set Books 1-7

HAPPY BEAR CAFE

COZY MYSTERY SERIES

Elected For Murder

Death And Decorations

Resolution for Revenge

To Kill A Rat

Sleeping Dogs Lie

A Bird In The Hand

Picture Perfect

Happy Bear Cafe Box Set Books 1-4

Happy Bear Cafe Box Set Books 5-7

Happy Bear Cafe Box Set Books 1-7

ANGELA CRAWFORD

COZY MYSTERY SERIES

Forest For The Trees

Put Your Affairs in Order

A Snake In The Grass

He Loves Me He Loves Me Not

Proof Is In the Printing

Deck The Walls

Angela Crawford Box Set Books 1-3

Angela Crawford Box Set Books 4-6

Angela Crawford Box Set Books 1-6

To get PBodi's latest releases at the lowest price sign up for her newsletter:

http://www.pbodi.com/p/newsletter.html

MIDSUMMER MURDER

P BODI
MOTHER EARTH'S KITCHEN
Midsummer Murder
MOTHER EARTH'S KITCHEN
COZY MYSTERY SERIES

CHAPTER ONE

The boom of the fireworks echoed against the mountains as the explosives rained down in brilliant shades of blue, orange, and red. The people of Elkridge oohed and aahed, thrilled to see the that the annual Fourth of July display was just as good as it had been last year. The entire production took place in the expansive Elkridge Park, a remarkably flat piece of ground that held a soccer field, baseball diamond, and a large playground. Most of the residents walked to the celebration, but cars from those who lived outside city limits could be seen stretching away from the park on every side road and alley way.

Violet Harris, owner of an organic grocery store called Mother Earth's Kitchen, sat on a blanket next to her best friend Maura. The two of them, just like the rest of the town, were happy to continue the midsummer tradition that brought the whole population out every year.

"I wonder how much they spend on this," Maura remarked, her straight and shiny hair reflecting the bursts of light in the sky. "I mean, I'm sure these things aren't cheap, and then there's got to be some sort of insurance premium the city pays in case anything happens."

Violet laughed. "I'm starting to think your mind revolves solely around money."

Her friend shrugged, not ashamed to admit it. As the manager of the local bank, it was part of her life. "Well, I'm surrounded by it all day. It's like the figures just get into my head and then I can't get them out. I can't tell you how many times a customer has come to me, angry because the amount in their checkbook register doesn't match what our systems say, and I just want to offer to balance their checkbook for them."

"You can come and do the books for Mother Earth's Kitchen any time you want to," Violet promised as another spray of fireworks lit up the mountains. "I'm pretty sure that's my least favorite part of it all."

The finale began, cutting off any hope of further conversation. Rockets volleyed one after another into the sky, creating a constant stream of explosions. When it was finally over, the residents cheered and clapped. Unlike other Independence Day celebrations Violet had been to before, where the residents filtered off back to their homes for their own private parties, the folks of Elkridge stuck around for live music and food from numerous vendors.

"You hungry?" Maura asked as she stood up and stretched.

Violet gladly unfolded her own body and stretched out the cramps that came from sitting on the ground for an hour. "Always. Let's go see what we can find."

Kevin, the owner of the Wildflower Inn, had set up a booth for his restaurant. He offered gourmet hot dogs, hamburgers made of black angus beef and topped with bleu cheese, and even steaks off a grill he was manning himself. Dressed in his usual attire of expensive and immaculate cowboy clothing, he greeted her enthusiastically when they made their way to the front of the line. "Hey, Violet! I thought you might start up a booth of your own this year."

Violet shook her head. "I'd rather sit back and enjoy the festivities," she said. "But it looks like you're getting plenty of business." The crowd behind them was surging forward, the people eager to get the best food before their favorite vendors ran out. "Although it might have been safer on the other side of the table. I'll take a veggie kabob."

"A hot dog and some home fries for me," Maura said, fishing cash out of her pocket. "And it's all on me."

The grocer knew better than to argue with her friend. She and Maura often exchanged meals back and forth without keeping track of who owed who or whose turn it was to buy. It worked well for them, but they had been friends since first grade.

The two women made their way over to the condiment cart, where an old man stooped over a dispenser and measured the precise amount of ketchup he needed onto his hot dog.

"Hi, Mr. Finley," Violet said as Maura busied herself with decorating her own hot dog. "How are things going down at the pharmacy?"

Mr. Finley straightened up slowly. The local pharmacist looked at Violet with cloudy blue eyes made huge by his thick glasses. His white hair stood out from his head like a mad scientist's, but Violet had been watching this man count out pills and measure out bubblegum-flavored liquid behind the counter of Finley's Pharmacy since she was a little kid. He was a patient and precise man who always had lollipops in the pocket of his lab coat.

"Well, things are getting ready to slow down quite a bit for me," he answered in his shaking voice. "I'm handing the drug store down to my grandson."

He gestured to the other side of the cart at a man in his mid-twenties. His brown hair was cropped short, and he had blue eyes that must have been the youthful version of Mr. Finley's. He kept his back straight and his shoulders wide, a stance that dripped confidence. "Hi there, I'm Chip Finley. I don't believe we've met."

Violet shook the hand he held out. "No, I don't believe we have. I haven't seen you around the pharmacy."

The young man shrugged and grinned. "I grew up in Aspen, but I made trips here every summer to stay with Granddad. I went to school for pharmacy at the University of Colorado, but

I also took quite a few business and financial courses. I knew that whether I ended up taking over the store or not, I wanted to know how to make and manage money."

Violet blinked, surprised at getting Chip's life history immediately upon meeting him. "Well, I'm sure you'll be very happy learning the ropes from your grandfather."

Chip shook his head. "I think the old man might have a thing or two to learn from me."

"Just ignore him," Mr. Finley said with a smirk on his wrinkled face. "He's just all fancy because he's been off to college."

But the young man was not one to be discouraged. "Just wait and see. I've got some big ideas for that little place."

Violet felt as though she was stepping right in on their family drama, and it was time to make her excuses. "Well, I've got to be getting along, but I'm sure I'll see you two around. Have a Happy Fourth!"

∼

iolet caught up with Maura just a few yards away, who was chatting with two young girls. From the stiff set of Maura's spine, Violet could tell that she was getting irritated. "Violet, let me introduce you to my newest employee. This is Erin Coville. I just hired her a few weeks ago as a teller."

The bank manager gestured to one of the girls in front of her. She had long red hair and bright green eyes that shone even in the dimly lit park. Erin wore far more makeup than a girl her age probably needed, and she smiled prettily at Violet. "Hi!" she squeaked as she wiggled her fingers. I'm Erin. I've heard all about you. You run the grocery store, right? I love your hair; I could give you some great pointers on taming those curls."

Violet widened her eyes slightly and bit her tongue. The girl spoke so quickly and changed subjects so rapidly that it was like an assault from her mouth. "Oh, um, thanks. It's nice to meet you. How are you enjoying your work at the bank?"

Erin flung her smooth hair over her shoulder and batted her mascara-coated eyelashes. "Well you see, I'm going to college for finance right now. I've already learned *loads* from my uncle, who runs an investment firm in Boulder, so college is just a formality, you know? I'll be running my own bank before you know it."

Nodding, Violet wondered if Erin could tell that the smile on her face was "just a formality" as well, because she certainly wasn't enjoying this conversation. Kaitlyn, one of the other tellers at the First Bank of Elkridge, stood next to Erin with her arms crossed and rolled her eyes.

Maura told the girls she would see them the next day at work, and she and Violet made their way back across the park to their blanket, where they could sit down and enjoy their meal.

"It sounds as though we have some energetic young entrepreneurs in Elkridge," Violet remarked, "but I think they might be a little bit too enthusiastic."

"Tell me about it." Maura rolled her eyes in much the same fashion as Kaitlyn had. "Have you met the new manager of the Antler Hotel yet?"

Violet pulled a chunk of yellow squash off her kabob and popped it in her mouth. It was just the right amount of salty and crispy. "What? No, I didn't even realize that had happened."

"It's a new thing," Maura replied as she wiped a bit of ketchup off her lip. "And from what I understand, the new manager is best friends with the pharmacist's grandson. The two of them met in college, and the friend followed him up here to take advantage of the business opportunity."

"Huh." Violet pulled off a mushroom and studied its perfect form for a minute before biting into it. "Have you met him? Is he half as obnoxious as Chip Finley?"

Maura's quirked her dark eyebrows at her friend. "Maybe even more so. He came into the bank last week to set up an account. He wouldn't stop talking about how his buddy Chip had given him all this amazing financial advice and how he's going to be a mountain hotel mogul before he turns thirty. Erin, of course, was practically drooling on the counter while she listened to him."

"Well, she does already know everything there is to possibly know about finance," Violet countered. "What made you hire her, anyway?"

Maura shrugged. "I was short a teller after Jeanette decided not to come back from maternity leave, and there weren't very many people who applied. Nobody wants to work Saturdays, for one thing. I needed a warm body to operate the teller window."

"I hate to tell you this, but she's kind of terrible. I hope she at least is good at her job."

The bank manager tipped her hand back and forth in the air. "So-so. I can't expect too much just yet, since she's new. And she's definitely ambitious. She told me in her interview that she'll work all the hours she can get."

Violet wiped her hands on a paper napkin. "Good. Good employees are hard to come by."

"Speaking of, where are yours?" Maura looked around the park for a sign of the other two that worked at Mother Earth's Kitchen. "I don't think I've seen them this evening."

"Carly is with Zach, which is no surprise. The two of them have been inseparable since they started dating. And I believe Rex is hanging out with Jamie."

"Is that the girl he goes hiking with?" Maura asked. "It sounds like you should have a better date for this shindig than me. What about Officer North? I'm sure he's around here somewhere tonight."

Violet glared at her best friend. "Shut up."

CHAPTER THREE

*V*iolet hustled up the street the next evening, hoping she would get to the bank before they closed. Most of the time, she sent Rex or Carly to do the nightly deposit so she could work on inventory or payroll, but Rex was off and Carly was dying to leave so she could get ready for her date that night with Zach. Violet had nearly forgotten about it until it was almost too late.

She burst in through the glass doors of the First Bank of Elkridge and trotted right up to the teller line. The clock on the wall above the drive-thru window told her she had made it with just five minutes to spare, and the name plaque on the counter told her that she was at Erin's window. The girl sauntered in from a side room and seated herself confidently on the stool before smiling and saying hello. She had the kind of attitude that said her customers should be honored to be served by her.

"Hi, Erin. I'm sorry to come rushing in here so late." Violet put the deposit bag on the counter and pushed it slightly forward. "I hate to do that to you."

"Oh, that's no problem." Erin picked up the bag, slowly unzipped it, and began taking clips of money out and setting them on the counter one at a time. "I can handle it."

"Have you guys been busy today?" Violet asked politely. She always liked to make small talk when she waited on her deposit. It made her feel less awkward than just standing there and watching someone count money.

But Erin was too busy frowning at the deposit ticket to pay attention. "What does this number say?" She pointed to the figure that denoted the total amount of checks in the deposit. "I can't quite read it."

Violet read the number to her and apologized. "Sorry, sometimes my handwriting gets a little messy at the end of the day."

Erin arched a copper eyebrow at her customer. "I have to make sure things are completely accurate, you know. I can't send anything to the vault if it isn't balanced correctly."

Violet *did* know that, and she resented the girl for acting as though she didn't. But she held her tongue as she watched Erin casually count out each bill just like she had all the time in the world and the bank wasn't about to close. At one point, her long, loose hair flopped forward over her shoulder. It landed on a clip of twenties and swept them right off the counter. Erin retrieved them and continued counting, only to have another hank of hair reach out and try to grab a stack of dollar bills. Violet fidgeted, worried that the new teller would end up losing half of her store's deposit. After several counts and recounts, with the teller alternately frowning at her calculator and her computer monitor, Erin was finally able to hand Violet a receipt. The grocer nearly snatched it out of the young girl's fingers.

The clock on the wall now showed that it was five minutes past closing time. The other teller on duty had closed the shades over the drive-thru window and was shutting down her computer. The loan officers on the other side of the lobby were chatting about their dinner plans, picking up their purses, and pushing in their chairs. Erin, however, seemed entirely unaffected. She calmly placed the money in her drawer and smile beatifically at Violet.

She took the opportunity to apologize once again, even though she knew the transaction wouldn't have taken nearly as long in more capable hands. "I really am sorry to come in here so late. I've kept you past your normal time."

Erin flipped her red hair back over her shoulder and stuck her chin just slightly in the air. "It's not a problem. I would stay here as late as Maura needed me to. I, unlike some people, am dedicated to my job." She cast a sideways glance at her fellow clerk, but the other girl either didn't hear Erin or was already getting used to ignoring her. "Besides, I'm not going home after work. I have a date with Billy Irving."

Violet didn't think Erin should have such a haughty look on her face when announcing that fact. Billy Irving had at one point been interested in Carly. When it didn't work out and Carly began dating Zack, Billy decided to take out his revenge by posting nasty comments and a bad review on the Facebook page for Mother Earth's Kitchen. Violet hadn't pursued the matter, since Billy had stopped his maligning actions once he was found out. Still, she didn't harbor any warm and cozy feelings toward him.

But she plastered a fake smile on her face that she hoped looked at least somewhat genuine. "Well, you two have fun."

On her way out the door, she took a deep breath and rolled her eyes. The girl was almost intolerable. Violet would have to remember to tell Maura about it the next time they saw each other, since the bank manager was already off work for the evening.

As Violet crossed a side road on her way back home, she was too busy fuming over Maura's terrible employee to notice the silver sedan that was swinging quickly off the main road. It nearly hit her as it swung onto the side street.

"Hey!" But the windows were rolled up on the car, and the driver was oblivious. It zoomed on past her toward the bank parking lot, which was behind the building. It careened into a parking spot at the very back of the lot, but nobody got out right away. Violet stared at it for only a moment before resuming her walk. She didn't have time to track people down and give them driving lessons. It was probably just Billy Irving, borrowing his parents' car and eager to pick up his date.

~

CHAPTER FOUR

By the next morning, Violet had forgotten completely about her incident at the bank. Rex and Carly were both scheduled to work that day, and she wouldn't have to deal with the newest teller at the First Bank of Elkridge. She had bigger fish to fry, including ordering signs for next week's sale on avocados and blackberries, entering her employees' time cards into the system, and of course the day to day management of the store.

Her cell phone chirped from the coffee table in her upstairs apartment, where she was just pulling a brush through her tangle of curly hair. She scooped it up and was surprised to see Maura's number. Her friend didn't usually call so early. "Well, good morning," she asked apprehensively, hoping everything was all right.

"Morning! Hey, do you wanna do lunch today?" Maura's voice was bright and chipper as ever; she must have already had plenty of coffee. "I think I'll have time if you're up for it."

Violet shrugged, even though Maura couldn't see her. "I don't see any reason why not. I'm fully staffed today. Where do you want to go?"

The sound of Maura's heels on the concrete and the jingling of her keys could be heard over the phone; she was getting ready to unlock the bank. "I'm thinking Mexican. I've been craving some…That's weird."

"What?" Violet put the phone on speaker so she could tame her curls into a long braid down her back.

"The door is already unlocked, but there's nobody here yet. I told the tellers I would open early since I had some work I wanted to come in and get done. Huh."

Violet's heart rose into her throat. "Maybe you shouldn't go in there. What if someone's broken in? I'll hang up so you can call the police."

"Don't you dare do any such thing," Maura admonished. "I don't need your handsome policeman to come and save me. I'm a lot more angry than I am scared." Several beeps came through the phone. "It looks like the alarm system was never even set last night."

Violet paused from securing an elastic band around the bottom of her braid. "Uh oh."

"Uh oh is right. Someone is going to be in a heck of a lot of trouble." Maura's shoes clicked on the tile floor as she explored the building. "The vault is still closed, and it doesn't look like anything is out of place. My guess is that they just didn't lock up properly when they left."

Though Erin had said she was going out on a date after work, Violet didn't want to incriminate the girl. After all, she hadn't been in any hurry to leave. It was better to let Maura sort out her employee issues before she said anything.

"Okay, I'm going to have to let you go. I need to call Erin and Michelle and see what happened last night. But I'll still meet you for lunch, okay?"

Violet hesitated. "Okay. But are you sure you're safe there?"

"Believe me, Violet. I'm ticked off enough right now that even if there were robbers in here, they wouldn't want to deal with me."

CHAPTER FIVE

When Maura plopped down in a seat across from Violet, it was apparent that she had been running herself ragged. Her hair, normally straight and neat without a strand out of place, was frizzy on top and needed a good brushing. Her mouth was a grim line, and her dark eyes stared somberly across the table at her friend. "You'll never believe the day I've had," she muttered, not even bothering to look at the menu the waiter set in front of her.

Violet raised an eyebrow over her limeade. "I take it there are some employees at the bank who are in hot water today."

Maura threw her hands in the air. "One of them is, but I can't seem to find the other one!

Erin and Michelle were supposed to close. When I called Michelle, she said she left Erin there by herself last night. The protocol is for the last two remaining people to leave together, but apparently she got tired of waiting on the leisurely Erin and went ahead and left."

"And Erin?" Violet asked. "She's not answering her phone?"

The banker shook her head and began munching on the chips and salsa on the brightly colored table. "Nope. I can't get a hold of her, her parents can't get a hold of her. Nobody has seen her since work yesterday. I've notified the police, but they haven't had any more luck than I have so far."

Violet took a chip for herself. "Don't they have to wait twenty-four hours before they can do anything?" she asked. She wondered if Maura had spoken to Officer North, but she didn't ask.

"I guess that isn't always true. If they have reasonable cause to believe something is wrong, they can take action."

Violet noted that her friend didn't bother taking a stab at her crush on the handsome officer, which could only mean that Maura was even more distraught than she looked. "You don't think she was waiting around to try to rob the bank, do you? I mean, I know she loves her job, but it seems that she also really loves money."

Maura ran her hands through her hair, making it even more disheveled than it already was. "It's funny you should ask that, because I had to count down her teller drawer this morning just as a precaution. Oddly enough, I couldn't find it at first. It turns out it had been left at her teller window unlocked. All of the money had been taken out of it, except for the special clip of bills that will set off an alarm."

The grocer pondered this as she took another chip and dunked it into the thin salsa. "Where should the drawer have been?"

"The teller cash drawers are all removable and go into the vault at the end of the night in special safety deposit boxes," Maura explained, leaning forward. "The inner vault is always locked, so Michelle left the main door to the vault open for Erin when she was done counting down her drawer. But evidently she never put her drawer in there or closed up the building." She pounded the table with her fist, making the salsa bowl jump slightly and slosh a drop over the rim. "I have to admit that I'm pretty ticked at

Michelle over this. I know that Erin isn't the most pleasant person to work with, but if she had just stuck around and waited then none of this ever would have happened. It's like I've got two tellers with completely different levels of experience that are both to blame."

"I'm sorry you're having to go through all of this. I wish I could help." She often ended up getting entangled in these sorts of things, and she was grateful that this one didn't involve her.

"Actually, you can," Maura said as she gratefully took a large margarita from the waiter. "I know; I shouldn't drink on my lunch hour, but today I think I deserve it. Anyway, I have to go to Erin's house this evening and see if she left her bank key there."

Sitting up straighter, Violet regarded the banker with surprised curiosity. She didn't like where this was going. "Why would you have to do that? Just make a new one when you get a new teller."

Maura sighed and sank a little deeper into the booth. "It's not that simple. If a key is lost, we have to rekey the entire bank. It's expensive, and quite frankly, a pain in the butt. If I'm lucky, Erin left her key at home and I can at least wrap up that part of things."

"Alright," Violet nodded her understanding. "So where do I come in?"

Her friend took a long drink of her margarita, the yellowish liquid descending visibly against the side of the glass. "Could you come with me? She lives with her parents, and I'm sure it's going to be this big sloppy mess of a thing. They'll either be sad or accusatory or I don't know what. But people like you. You make them feel comfortable. If you come along, maybe it will soften the blow of asking them to look through their daughter's things for a dumb key."

Nodding grimly, Violet agreed. "I can do that. I don't really have much else going on after work." But she wished that she did. This wasn't going to be a fun task.

~

CHAPTER SIX

*V*iolet's stomach squirmed inside her as she and Maura stood on the front porch of Mr. and Mrs. Coville's house. It was a nice home with clean white siding, dark green shudders, and faux columns along the covered porch. It didn't look like the sort of place where one would expect to find a girl who had either robbed the local bank or been abducted while someone else did it.

Mr. Coville opened the door after the first knock. Maura had called ahead, and he must have been standing by the window waiting for them. He was a man in his late forties with a ring of gray hair around his head where he hadn't already gone bald. Numerous worry lines creased his forehead, and he gazed at Maura with pitiful brown eyes. "Ms. Turner," he said with a nod before turning to Violet with a curious gaze. Instead of asking who she was, he stepped back and opened the door wider for the two of them to enter.

"Please sit down." Mr. Coville gestured to a formal sitting room just off the entryway, complete with wing-backed chairs, a vintage sofa with wood trim, and a large area rug on the wooden floor.

A woman came in from the back of the room bearing a tea tray. It was obvious from her vivid red hair and her bright green eyes that this was Erin's mother. A few streaks of white broke up her auburn mane, but otherwise her daughter looked remarkably like her. She had the same careworn look on her face as her husband did, and she seated herself quietly on one end of the sofa after offering a teacup to each of her guests.

"I'd like to start," Mr. Coville said, "by letting you know that we want to do everything we can to assist you. We don't know what Erin may or may not have done, but we do know that we want her back."

Violet swallowed a lump of guilt. The man, in his grief, might not have completely understood

Maura's mission here. There was little that either of the two women could do that would locate their daughter.

"I don't know how much help I'll be in that department," Maura said, reflecting Violet's private thoughts. "But of course everyone at the bank will cooperate fully with the police, and I do hope that you get some answers soon." She set her teacup on the coffee table and folded her hands primly in her lap. Her hair had been restored sometime during the afternoon to its usual state of tidiness, and she once again looked like the in-charge bank manager that Violet knew so well. "I've come here this afternoon first to extend to you my sympathy. Even if Erin has simply run off on a spontaneous vacation, I'm sure it has caused you great distress."

"Oh, but Erin wouldn't do something like that," Mrs. Coville interrupted. Her voice was quiet and wispy, the complete opposite of her daughter's. "She isn't flighty like that. She always lets us know where she is and who she's with. We trust her implicitly."

Maura nodded, though Violet could see by the stiffness in her muscles that she was extremely uncomfortable with the situation. "I'm sure that's true, which only makes my job all the more difficult. You see, I've come to ask you if Erin has left her bank keys here. I know it seems like a cold-hearted task, but the bank needs to have them back if at all possible."

Mr. Coville nodded as though he expected this. "Darling, go get her keys, will you?" Mrs. Coville scowled for a moment, but she stood and retreated from the room. Her husband turned back to the two women once she was gone. "I don't know what the keys looks like, but you're welcome to look through them. For what it's worth, I'm sorry that our Erin has caused such trouble for you. I can't help but hope that none of this was her fault, but I also know that isn't necessarily a logical thought."

"It's quite all right, Mr. Coville," Maura assured him. "I also hope that this wasn't her doing. She's new and still learning the ropes at the bank, but it's obvious that she's a very driven young girl."

This was a very polite way of putting it, Violet thought, but the compliment visibly eased the mind of the missing girl's father.

Mrs. Coville returned, bearing a heavy set of keys adorned with a long purple lanyard and several keychains of various animals and fluffy things. Maura took the clanking heap of metal from her and carefully sifted through each key. "I don't see anything on here that looks right. My tellers usually keep their bank keys separate from their car keys, because they must keep them close while they're at work. Does Erin have any other keys I can look at?"

Erin's father, his brow even more furrowed than it had been when Violet and Maura had arrived, nodded and stood. "Why don't you come and look in her room? We don't know what we're looking for, and it might be quicker if you just take a peek."

"Albert..." Erin's mother nearly growled as she spoke her husband's name.

"It'll be fine, Marsha."

Maura handed the keys to Mrs. Coville as she stood to follow the man to another part of the house. The woman took them with a frown, then turned her bleak look to Violet. "Who are you, anyway?"

Violet jumped a little at finally being addressed. "My name is Violet Harris. I run Mother Earth's Kitchen here in Elkridge. Maura and I are best friends." She continued to follow

Mr. Coville and Maura down a hallway as she introduced herself.

"Well, what do you have to do with it then?" The woman's frown deepened.

It was a fair question, but Violet felt that Mrs. Coville could have spoken in a friendlier manner. Still, her daughter was missing, and perhaps that made people's manners fly out the window. "Maura and I are best friends. This is a tough time for everyone right now, and I'm sure most of all for you."

Fortunately, their conversation was cut off by their entrance into Erin's room. The teller enjoyed a very feminine décor, with froths of white lace covering the bed, a fluffy pink area rug, and numerous stuffed animals.

"Feel free to look around," Mr. Coville said as he gestured around the room. "Erin didn't have anything to hide."

~

CHAPTER SEVEN

Maura stepped tentatively up to a desk in the corner covered with glittery stationery and a few scattered books. Violet remained by her side, more to avoid further conversation with Erin's mother than anything. She perused the multicolored pens and novelty shaped erasers before her eyes traveled to a notepad. It was small and thin and had nothing written on it other than the Antler Hotel letterhead. Violet raised her eyebrows but said nothing.

"The police have already been by," Mr. Coville explained. "They were very kind about things, listening to any detail that we might think was pertinent. I expected them to dismiss us since she hasn't been missing for all that long yet, but they were happy to help. I believe it was Officer North. Have you ever had dealings with him?"

Violet wondered if the Coville's realized that their daughter may have stolen a few thousand dollars' worth of cash out of her teller drawer, which would explain why the police were so interested. "Yes," she said instead, "he's helped me out a few times."

The women moved to a vanity, where several perfume bottles were scattered amongst various other hygiene debris. Right in front of the mirror, at the very center of the table, was a tiny bottle of lotion with the hotel's logo.

"I just really don't know what to make of everything," the man went on. "It's the sort of thing you see on television and think it will never happen to your family. But then it does…" He couldn't finish his sentence because he was too busy blinking back tears. Violet didn't blame him. "She has so much going on for her, you know? She's started college, and she gets excellent grades. Of course, we told her she could stay here for as long as she wants to so she wouldn't have to pay her living expenses while she's in school. She's very frugal, you know. And she was just starting to date that nice young man from the hotel."

"Billy works at the hotel now?" Violet asked, caught off guard. The last she knew, Billy Irving was in the construction business.

Mr. Coville gave her a blank look for a moment before he regained himself. "Um, no. Paul Whittaker, the young man who manages the hotel now. He's a few years older than our Erin, but he seems like a respectable young man. He even came over and had dinner with us before ever taking her out."

"He *is* a little boastful, though," Mrs. Coville sniffed.

This time it was Mr. Coville's turn to admonish his spouse. "Marsha…"

But she set her shoulders and pointed her chin in the air, a stance that only further reflected the family resemblance between herself and her daughter. "Well, he is. All he wanted to talk about were his investments he made under his friend's advice, that Chip Finley who's taking over the pharmacy. Maybe if he hadn't intrigued her with all that fancy finance talk, our daughter would be here in her room where she belongs."

A heavy tension settled over the room and

sagged onto Violet's shoulders. She had largely been ignoring the couple as they recounted the endless details about Erin's disappearance, but something about the tone of Marsha Coville's voice when she spoke about the would-be hotel magnate made her ears perk up. She tore her eyes from the surface of the night stand she had been examining and turned to Erin's parents. "Are you saying he has something to do with his disappearance?"

"No." Mr. Coville's response was instant and firm. "That's not what she's saying at all."

"But he could have." The quiet Mrs. Coville was no longer content to let her husband run the show. "That's what they always find out when sweet girls like our Erin go missing. There's always a man involved, luring her away from her family and everything she loves until suddenly she's missing or dead. You can't deny that, Albert. You've said the same thing yourself when we've watched those crime documentaries."

"That's different, Marsha, and I don't think this is a debate to be held in front of our guests." He put his hands on his wife's shoulders and steered her toward the door before he turned to

Maura and Violet. "You ladies do what you need to do. Feel free to look in her drawers or her closet. We'll be waiting for you in the parlor."

CHAPTER EIGHT

Half an hour later, Violet gratefully sank into the cool leather interior of Maura's red sports car. They had half-heartedly perused Erin's things to no avail, and then of course they had to sit down and listen to Mr. Coville regale them with proud parenting moments while Mrs. Coville made snide remarks about the bad influence of the male gender.

"That was…interesting," Maura remarked as the engine roared to life and they swept out of the Coville's driveway. "They were a lot more cooperative than I would have expected anyone to be."

Violet nodded. "Almost a little too cooperative. Why would they let two practical strangers sift through their daughter's belongings?"

Maura lifted one hand off the steering wheel so she could shake her finger at her friend. "Don't start playing sleuth on me again. I never should have dragged you into this."

"But you did," Violet reminded her. "Now explain to me their weird behavior."

"Maybe they're just weird people?" Maura suggested with a shrug. "Erin isn't exactly normal herself. Besides, they want to find their daughter. If I was in their shoes, I'd probably let strangers in my house to look around, too."

Violet watched the trees that lined the mountain road fly by. "There are too many things here that don't add up."

"I don't think there's very much that will add up until they find Erin." She turned the car onto Main Street and slowed down. "It's no mystery that it's a mystery."

But Violet wasn't ready for her ideas to be dismissed so easily. "Okay, but think about this: Erin's cash drawer was empty when you got to the bank. That makes it look like she stole the money. But she was incredibly meticulous about counting up my deposit the other night; so much so I thought she would never get it done. Someone who's so concerned about making her drawer balance isn't going to turn around and take all the cash with her when she leaves. Or if she did, she would have some way of covering it up."

Maura nodded, conceding to Violet's point. "That makes sense, but it isn't any real proof. I could just as easily argue that she was particular about your deposit because she didn't want anyone to suspect her before she was ready to make her move."

"Okay, then take this into consideration: You told me how fascinated Erin was with the new manager of the Antler Hotel. What's his name again?"

"Paul. Paul Whittaker."

"Yeah, that guy. So she must have had something going on with him judging by what her parents said and the fact that she had lotion and a notepad from the hotel in her room. But when I talked to her at the bank, she said she had a date that night with Billy Irving." Violet was getting excited, talking faster the more she went on. She wasn't sure where it was all leading, but it had to mean something. She just hadn't put the pieces of the puzzle together yet.

Maura pulled up in front of Mother Earth's Kitchen and turned off the car. "She's a young girl. As far as I know, she's not in a committed relationship. Maybe she's dating both of them."

Violet rolled her eyes. "I can't say that I've met this Paul Whittaker, but you know how I feel about Billy Irving."

Sitting against the back of the seat and sighing, Maura agreed. "I know. But that doesn't mean she felt the same way. As annoying as she can be, she's a pretty girl. Guys like her. I've seen plenty of them hitting on her in the short time she's been working for me."

"I wonder which one nearly ran me over on his way to pick her up from work," Violet retorted. "But I couldn't see the driver and I didn't get a plate. It might have been someone who had nothing to do with Erin." Her excitement was beginning to wane. Maura was right. None of this was any real proof or evidence that she could turn in to the police or use to find out what happened.

But Maura had a red fingertip to her lips. "That's interesting. Maybe I can check the tapes and see if anything shows up. But the cameras only point at certain areas of the bank and the parking lot."

Violet almost jumped out of her seat. "I can't believe I didn't think to ask you about that! Didn't the security cameras show whether or not Erin left the bank? Or who she might have left with?"

"I'm afraid not." Maura turned the corners of her mouth down gravely. "Someone turned them off after Michelle left."

Swinging open the car door, Violet got out and turned back to her friend. "I'm sorry. Let me know if there's anything else I can do."

Maura waited while Violet unlocked the door, let herself into the store, and locked the door behind her before zooming off toward her own house.

~

CHAPTER NINE

"Where do you want me to put the display of apricots? The produce section is kind of overflowing right now, and I don't know if I should make room by the front windows or just stuff them in a basket near the door."

Violet didn't hear Carly's question. She was too busy running over numerous scenarios in her mind, trying to figure out just what happened to Erin Coville. Every time she rang up a customer, she tried to wrap her head around the financial aspect of the mystery. In the meat department, where some Bison meat had dripped blood onto the floor, she wondered where Erin was and if she was still alive. She studied a young man who came in to buy a jar of organic peanut butter, speculating over whether he had ever asked Erin out on a date.

"Or I could just set them out on the sidewalk with a sign that says, 'Free, please take one.'" Carly put her hand on her hip and waved the other one in front of Violet's face. "Earth to Violet. Come in, Violet."

The grocer blinked and focused on her employee. "I'm sorry. My head is really in the clouds today. What did you need?"

Carly shook her head. "Don't worry about it. I'll figure it out. Are you sure you're okay?"

Violet swept a hand over her forehead and leaned on the counter. "I just have a lot on my mind, thanks."

The bell over the door signaled a new customer, and the young man who came in looked the same way that Violet felt. His short blonde hair stuck out in several directions, and he had enormous dark circles under his eyes. He was dressed in a button-down shirt and khakis, and he might have looked nice if his shirt hadn't been halfway untucked and his pants wrinkled. His general state of dishabille and the paleness of his skin suggested that he had slept in his clothes, restlessly.

Violet watched as he wandered through the store, picking up a few random items here and there. He didn't bother with a shopping basket, but attempted to hold it all in his arms at once. This method only worked for the first few items; he kept dropping them after that. Rushing to him with a basket, Violet felt compelled to be kind to this poor man. "Hello. I don't think I've seen you around town before. I'm Violet Harris, the owner of the store."

He poured his items into the basket and gave her a wan smile. "Thank you. I'm Paul Whittaker, the new manager of the Antler Hotel. I just got into town a few weeks ago."

"Oh, yes. I've heard of you." Violet would have handed him the basket, but he didn't look as though he was capable of holding it. Was he in this state because he had done something terrible to Erin and couldn't quite live with himself? "I understand you made some good investments that allowed you to take over the hotel. That's impressive."

Paul shrugged. "I think that might be the only thing going right in my life. I was dating this sweet girl from the bank, but now she's turned up missing. It wasn't like we were going steady or anything, but I was pretty crazy about her. Now I'm so worried, I can't even sleep." He swiped both hands down his face, blinking rapidly. "I'm sorry. I don't know why I just told you all of that."

"It's quite alright. It happens all the time." Maura hadn't been wrong when she said Violet made people feel comfortable, but she liked to attribute it to the cozy feeling of the store with it's warm wooden floors and timber frame beams. She guided Paul to the herbal tea section. "Why don't we scoop up some loose-leaf tea that will help you relax tonight and maybe get some sleep? On the house."

As she opened a small bag and took the lid off the container of chamomile tea, Violet wondered at herself. Just last evening she had been ready to accuse him of murder, abduction, bank robbery, or all three based solely on his fling with Erin. Actually meeting him, though, had made her change her mind completely. He had a nice energy about him despite his exhaustion.

The doorbell rang again, and Violet peeked around the display to welcome the new customer. But it was Officer North, and the leaden expression on his face was all business.

His dark eyes skimmed the store, locking on hers for just a moment before they landed on Paul Whittaker, causing his shoulders to sag ever so slightly. The policeman strode across the store with such authority that even Violet wanted to skitter off into the back room.

"Paul Whittaker?" he asked the young man.

"Yes, sir," came the shaky reply.

Officer North avoided looking at Violet, keeping his gaze steadily on Paul. "I need you to come down to the station with me for questioning."

"Oh. Um. Okay." Paul looked at the basket with his few groceries and the tea that Violet was in the middle of putting together.

"I can hold onto all of this for you," Violet assured him. None of it was perishable, and the miserable look in his deep brown eyes made her feel sorry for him. He would definitely be getting a discount when the police were done with him.

Paul nodded numbly and took a step away from the tea display. "They've already asked me about Erin. Did something else happen?"

The detective's gaze flicked to Violet for just a moment, as if he didn't want to say what he had to say in front of her. But Paul made no move to leave the store just yet, hanging just a foot behind Violet as he waited for the answer to his question.

"Erin's body has been found," Officer North said quietly, "in the field behind the hotel."

As pale as he already was, the color drained from Paul's skin even more as he leaned heavily on the tea counter. "Oh, my goodness." His face crumpled for a moment, but he forced himself to stand up and follow the lawman out the door.

Violet couldn't move, watching dumbly as poor Paul left. She hadn't missed the tears that were forming in his eyes, held back only by his rapid blinking. Nor did she miss the dark look that Officer North shot at her over his shoulder. She didn't need to ask him to know what it meant: Something bad had happened, and she was already getting too involved. Her head began to pound.

CHAPTER TEN

The clock on the back wall of the store ticked more and more slowly as the day wore on. The basket of goods that Violet had saved behind the counter for Paul as promised had not been retrieved. Every time the door opened, the grocer turned to it hopefully. She shouldn't care so much about what happened to a stranger, but she liked the young entrepreneur. If the circumstances had been different, she was sure they would have gotten along quite well.

To make matters worse, her headache had yet to subside. She squinted at the figures on the cash register, uncertain that she was seeing them correctly. The pain behind her eyes was making her vision blur, and her stomach roiled with nausea. Even a steaming mug of Feverfew tea didn't help.

The store wasn't too busy, and Violet was ready to give up. "Carly, I'm running down to the pharmacy for a minute if you'll mind the store."

The blonde girl left the display of organic baby food she had been organizing and came up to the counter, her forehead wrinkled in concern. "Really?"

It was a fair question. Violet almost never turned to modern medicine for something that could be fixed at home. "Yeah. My head is killing me."

"You can go upstairs and lay down if you'd like," Carly offered.

But Violet knew that even if she did, she wouldn't be able to get her mind off Erin and Paul. A walk down to the drugstore would probably do her some good, and the medicine she bought there would make it even better. "That's alright. I won't be gone long."

Finley's Pharmacy wasn't exactly hopping on a midweek afternoon. The small store held no other customers when Violet walked in. She had hoped that old Mr. Finley would still be working, but his grandson Chip was the one on duty behind the counter. "Well if it isn't Violet Harris!" he boomed across the cramped space filled with boxes and bottles. "You've been causing an awful lot of trouble for me lately."

"I have?" Chip's voice had been far too loud, and it ricocheted around inside her head. "What have I done?" As far as she could remember, she hadn't seen him since the Fourth of July.

"It's that store of yours," he remarked with a smirk as she approached the counter. "Usually when people come in for prescriptions they pick up over-the-counter medications while they're here. That's a lot of how this store makes a profit. A sick customer is already here, so they buy their aspirin and a few other necessities instead of going somewhere else."

"And?" Violet didn't have the patience to listen to his business plan.

"And they all tell me that your herbs and teas work so well that they don't want to buy the manufactured pills we have in here." He held his arms wide, his lab coat hanging open as he gestured to the grandness of Finley's Pharmacy.

"I'm sorry." She wasn't really, but it was the thing to say. "Ironically, I'm here for some of your pills myself. My head is killing me."

Chip came out from behind the counter and strode confidently down one of the short aisles. "We have all of our painkillers over here. Do you prefer Aspirin, Acetaminophen, Naproxen Sodium, or Ibuprofen? Most of them come in either tablets or gel caps, and we have a few in liquid form as well."

Violet shook her head, then stopped herself. It only made the pain worse. "I don't know. Something mild, I guess. I usually do the same things my customers do and just drink a mug of tea."

Chip scooped up a bottle of Acetaminophen and returned to his station behind the counter of the dispensary. Shelves and shelves of prescription medications took up the space behind him, separated from the rest of the store by a glass wall. He set the bottle of pills on the counter and leaned forward conspiratorially. "You know, I can share some great investment opportunities with you if you'd like. I don't tell just anyone, but I'm sure you'd like to make some extra income on the side."

Mother Earth's Kitchen supplied Violet's needs nicely, but he piqued her curiosity. "Are these the same kinds of investments that Paul Whittaker made? I understand he did well."

The young pharmacist's face clouded over for just an instant. "No. I'm afraid he didn't listen to my advice, and he just got lucky."

"I see. Well, I think I've got my hands full enough as it is." Violet was ready to pay for the medicine and get back to her store. Chip wasn't as pleasant to deal with as Mr. Finley was.

Chip nodded and scanned the bottle. "I bet you do."

Fishing her wallet out of her purse, Violet said, "I'm sorry to hear about Erin. I'm sure it's difficult for you, since she was dating your good friend."

"What's that?" Chip asked. "Oh, right. The banker girl. I don't know. I didn't hang around with them very much. I'm busy enough as it is. Besides, I found her to be almost intolerable."

Violet studied the neutral expression on the man's face. "Still, it's got to be rough knowing that your good friend has been taken in for questioning." When Chip didn't reply, she continued. "You knew about that, right? And that they found her body?"

He gave her the total for her purchase before leaning forward again and looking her squarely in the eye. "It isn't really my business. Paul got in over his head, and it's not my job to worry about it."

"Oh. Okay." Violet watched in stunned silence as he bagged her purchase and ripped the receipt from the register. Any normal person would have at least been upset that their friend might be implicated in a murder. "Well, you have a nice day."

"Wait." Chip held the small bag, not letting Violet have it yet. "I have another opportunity I want to discuss with you. I act as a business consultant on the side. For a small fee, I can examine your business plan for your store, go over your profit and loss statements, and help you turn it into a real moneymaker."

Violet waved off his offer. "I appreciate it, but I think I'm doing alright—"

"Not as good as you could be," he interrupted. "If you just let me come in and take a look, I can show you."

"You certainly have a lot going on, don't you?" Violet asked. "You've mentioned your investments, and of course you have the pharmacy. Isn't that enough?"

That same dark look that had taken over his features when she had mentioned Paul Whittaker came back again. He slapped the bag down on the counter. "No." He turned away from her, ostensibly to work on filling prescriptions.

CHAPTER ELEVEN

Violet picked up the bag, grateful to be done with this miserable person and be back at her store, even with a headache. But just before she turned to leave, she noticed something marring the whiteness of his lab coat. A long red hair clung to the fabric, dangling down from the back of his shoulder.

"Oh, no," she muttered.

Chip whirled around, his lips curled into a snarl. "What? Is your headache medicine too processed for you?"

Taking one step back, Violet put her free hand to her mouth. It made sense, and yet it didn't. She couldn't possibly be right. But at least she was safely on the other side of the counter from the druggist. "You killed Erin, didn't you?

You needed the money, and you thought you could pull her into your scheme."

He took no time to answer, and he was too quick for Violet to react. His long arms reached over the counter and grabbed her by the shoulders. He yanked her over the laminate countertop, sending a display of lip balm flying. Violet tumbled to the floor in the dispensary.

Chip stood over her, his eyes wild and his breathing coming in great gulps. "Really?" he shouted. "Of all the people to figure me out it has to be some grocery store hippie? You've got to be kidding me?"

Violet didn't bother to answer, struggling instead to get to her feet. But Chip swept a foot underneath her arms and knocked her back to the floor. Several bottles of medicine rained down from the shelves, their lids popping open and scattering pills in every direction.

"It was bad enough that I had to kill her. I thought for sure she was smart enough to sneak a little money out of the bank here and there. You should have heard the way she bragged about her financial skills. But no. She swore she couldn't do it. I went in there that day just to talk to her. I had no idea that she would be there alone. And it was the perfect time! She could have done it so easily! But she refused, and things got out of hand." He was talking quickly, gesturing wildly with his hands. "I don't know what was wrong with her. She cooperated with me well enough at first, shutting down the security cameras and emptying her drawer. But she got all weird when she found out I had a gun. Maybe Paul had gotten into her head, or that grimy Billy guy she was interested in. I could have really taken her places, you know?"

He had been involved enough in his tirade that Violet had managed to get herself to a sitting position. She had banged into one of the metal shelves when she fell off the counter, and now her head pounded even harder than before. Every part of her body urged her to get up and try to run away. Every part except her head. Her vision was going dark around the edges. "Listen, Chip. It's your business. I won't tell anyone. I just need to go home." Violet grabbed the edge of a shelf, careless of the small boxes she knocked off with her fingers, and pulled herself to her feet.

"Oh no you don't!" Chip shoved her back down to the ground.

But he needn't have bothered. Violet's tunnel

vision had grown worse. She could only see what was in the very center of her gaze. She looked up helplessly at Chip, who stood over her, daring her to get back up again. Behind him, on the other side of the counter, was another face. It was someone she knew, but she couldn't find his name in her brain. The newcomer leapt over the counter easily, tackling Chip to the ground with a crash. Just before she blacked out completely, Violet remembered his name. "Billy Irving," she mumbled.

~

CHAPTER TWELVE

*V*iolet sat in the back of the ambulance and closed her eyes against the flashing lights that danced off the brick facades of the downtown buildings. Someone had tried to get her to lay down on the gurney, but she wanted to see what was going on even if she didn't quite understand it all. Her trip over the pharmacy counter had left her quite confused.

"I think it's mostly just scrapes and bruises," said the paramedic next to her. "I think your concussion is mild. To be sure, we'll need to take you to the hospital for an MRI."

Violet nodded her head in agreement, but she wasn't ready to go just yet. There was a small crowd of people waiting to talk to her. Mr. Finley stepped up to the back of the ambulance first.

"I'm so very sorry for all of this," the old man said, wringing his hands in front of him. "I'll do anything I can to make it up to you."

"It's not your fault," Violet assured him.

"And yet I'm so very ashamed. No grandson of mine should have behaved like that. I love this town and the people in it. If I had known, I never would have offered him the store." He reached out and patted her hand with his wrinkled hand before hobbling slowly off to the pharmacy, presumably to pick up the mess once the police were done with it.

Maura stepped up next, her eyes shining. "You're something else, you know? I know I said you shouldn't go play sleuth again, but I stand corrected. You saved an innocent man and sent the right one to jail. Although I think you might have come out of it a little worse for wear this time." She winced as she examined Violet's bruises. "How did you figure it out?"

Violet wanted to shrug, but it was too painful. "I don't really know anymore. It was his finances, and the hair on his coat." She sighed. She wasn't making any sense. "I'm not sure I even know what he did."

"I'm happy to fill in the details," Maura replied. "Our buddy Chip liked to brag about his financial know-how, but he sunk a ton of money into some investments that failed. He was desperate for new income to pay of his high credit card bills, so he tried to scheme Paul into making a fake investment. He didn't go for it, so Chip turned to Erin."

"And he thought he could get her to embezzle for him," Violet volunteered.

"Exactly. But our girl was too smart for that. Chip lost his temper and killed her, but he figured he could blame his former friend Paul. He probably could have, if you weren't around to stop him."

Violet waved off the compliment. "I think next time, I need to call out murderers over the phone or something. This is getting a bit painful."

Maura smiled. "I'm sorry. You get better, and don't worry about a thing. Rex and Carly are taking care of the store, and I'm on strict orders to keep them updated. I'll come see you at the hospital, okay?"

Before she could let the EMT know she was ready to go, one more person pushed through the crowd to see her. Violet's heart sank into her stomach at the sight of Officer North, but then she noticed that he no longer wore the hard look she had seen when he had come to find Paul Whittaker. Instead, his smile creased the corners of his dark eyes. He stood directly in front of her and laid a hand on her knee. Violet could smell his cologne.

"Next time something weird goes down in Elkridge," he said, "I'm not going to bother to look for clues. I won't interview anyone or do any other investigative techniques. I'll just follow you around until you lead me to the bad guy."

Violet smiled, grateful that at least he didn't seem to be angry with her for sticking her nose where it didn't belong once again. "You can do that if you like, but I'll be pretty boring."

Officer North's smile increased. "I can't think of anyone I'd rather spend my time with."

The End

To get Eve Craig's latest releases at the lowest price sign up for her newsletter: http://www.EveCraig.com/p/newsletter.html

ABOUT THE AUTHOR

Cozy Mystery writer P Bodi is a former investigator with an intense curiosity and obsession with dogs, and all other critters with fur, fins, or feathers.

As an avid reader she has a passion for writing books that will provide entertainment and escape for her readers with over 20 books currently in publication.

For a complete list of books by PBodi go to her website at www.PBodi.com and click on Book List.

To get PBodi's new releases at the lowest price sign up for her newsletter:
www.PBodi.com/p/newsletter.html

New Year's Resolution

The Heart Of The Murder

The Luck Of The Irish

A Corpse In The Kitchen

Midsummer Murder

Mother Earth's Kitchen Box Set Books 1-4

Mother Earth's Kitchen Box Set Books 5-7

Mother Earth's Kitchen Box Set Books 1-7

HAPPY BEAR CAFE

COZY MYSTERY SERIES

Elected For Murder

Death And Decorations

Resolution for Revenge

To Kill A Rat

Sleeping Dogs Lie

A Bird In The Hand

Picture Perfect

Happy Bear Cafe Box Set Books 1-4

Happy Bear Cafe Box Set Books 5-7

Happy Bear Cafe Box Set Books 1-7

ANGELA CRAWFORD

COZY MYSTERY SERIES

Forest For The Trees

Put Your Affairs in Order

A Snake In The Grass

He Loves Me He Loves Me Not

Proof Is In the Printing

Deck The Walls

Angela Crawford Box Set Books 1-3

Angela Crawford Box Set Books 4-6

Angela Crawford Box Set Books 1-6

To get PBodi's latest releases at the lowest price sign up for her newsletter:

http://www.pbodi.com/p/newsletter.html